IT MIGHT BE AN APPLE

SHINSUKE YOSHITAKE

 Thames & Hudson

On the table, there was an apple.

But wait a minute.
It might not be an apple at all...

It might be a huge cherry.

It might be filled with jelly.

It might be all peel
with no apple inside.

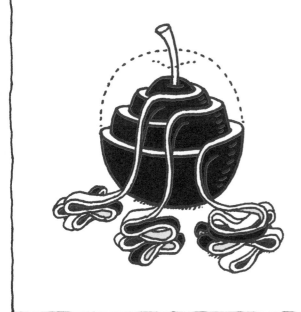

Or it might be half apple
and half orange.

It might be a red fish,
curled up into a ball.

It might be packed with clever devices...

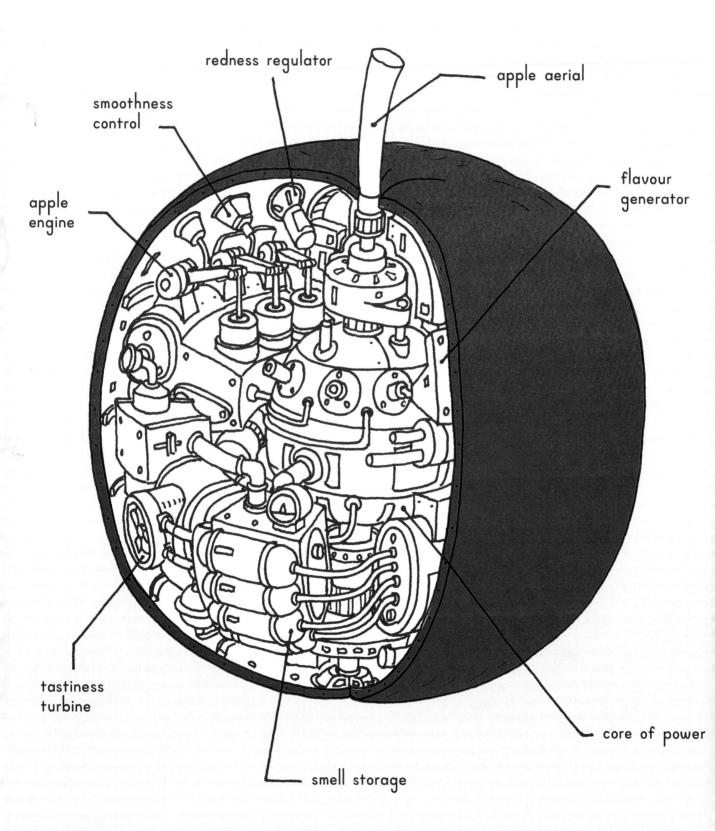

redness regulator

apple aerial

smoothness control

flavour generator

apple engine

tastiness turbine

smell storage

core of power

It might be an egg...

And when it hatches, the baby
might think I'm its mother.

If I water it every day, it might grow as big as a house.

day one

a week later

a month later

three months later

It might grow into the best house ever.
I could even eat the walls!

It might need a hat or a new hairstyle.

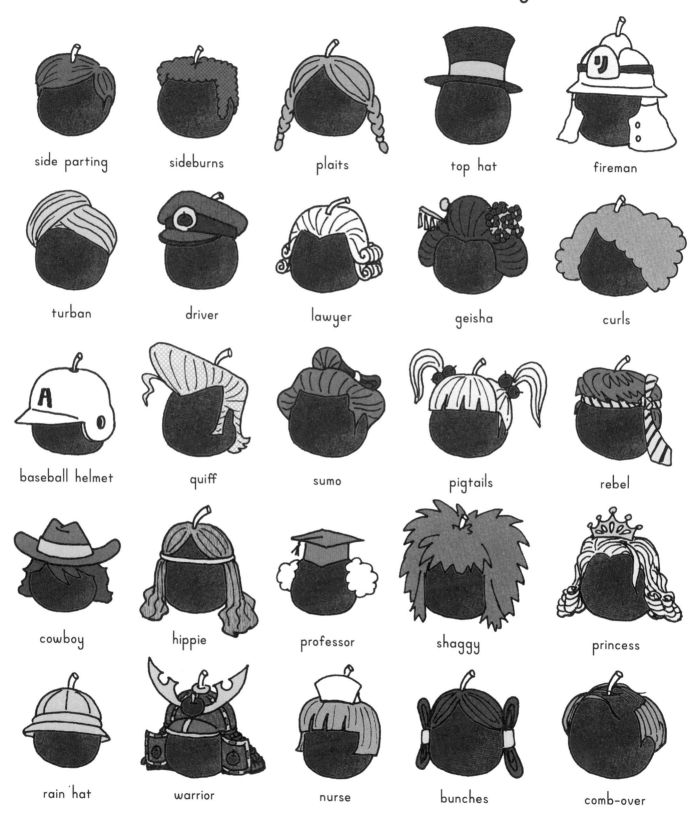

side parting

sideburns

plaits

top hat

fireman

turban

driver

lawyer

geisha

curls

baseball helmet

quiff

sumo

pigtails

rebel

cowboy

hippie

professor

shaggy

princess

rain hat

warrior

nurse

bunches

comb-over

It might wish it were something else.

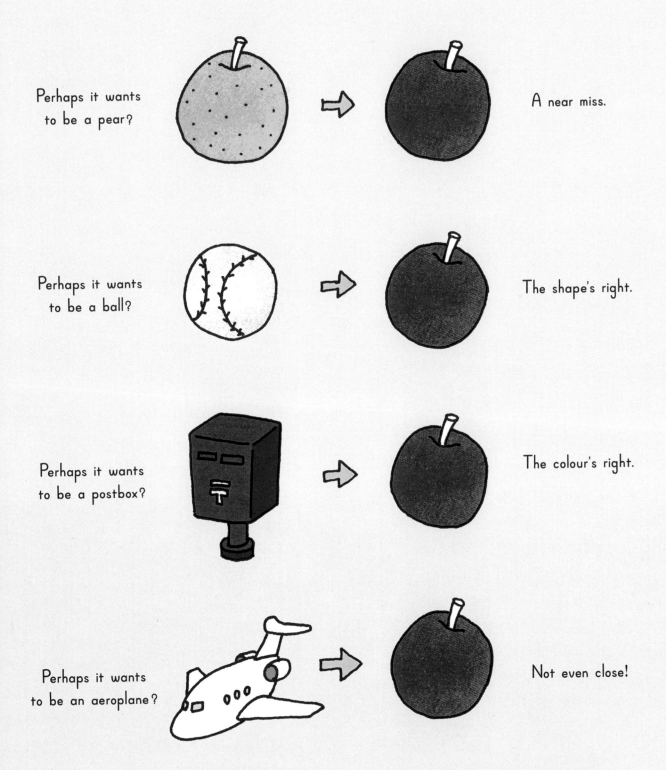

Perhaps it wants to be a pear? → A near miss.

Perhaps it wants to be a ball? → The shape's right.

Perhaps it wants to be a postbox? → The colour's right.

Perhaps it wants to be an aeroplane? → Not even close!

It might be a tiny little planet that fell to earth.

WHEE!

CRASH!

If I look very closely, the surface might be crawling with tiny aliens.

It might have feelings...

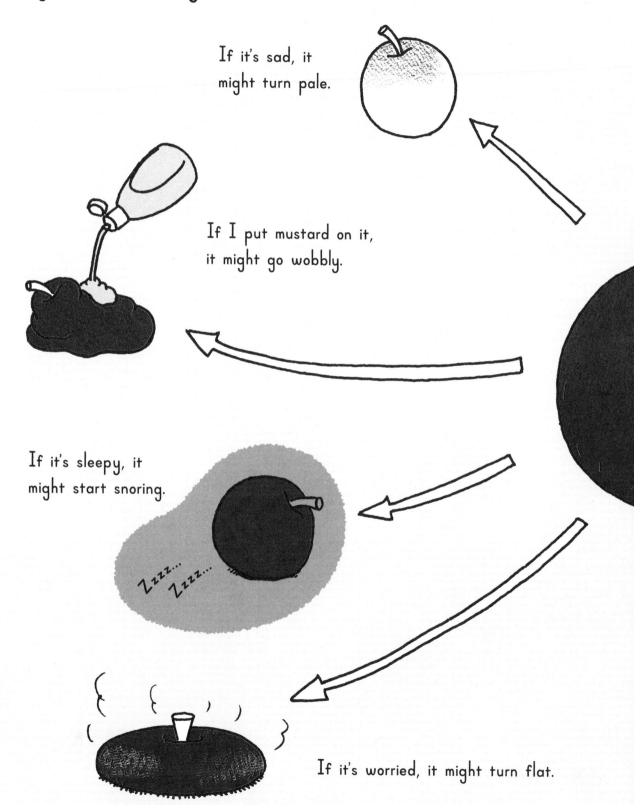

If it's sad, it might turn pale.

If I put mustard on it, it might go wobbly.

If it's sleepy, it might start snoring.

Zzzz... Zzzz...

If it's worried, it might turn flat.

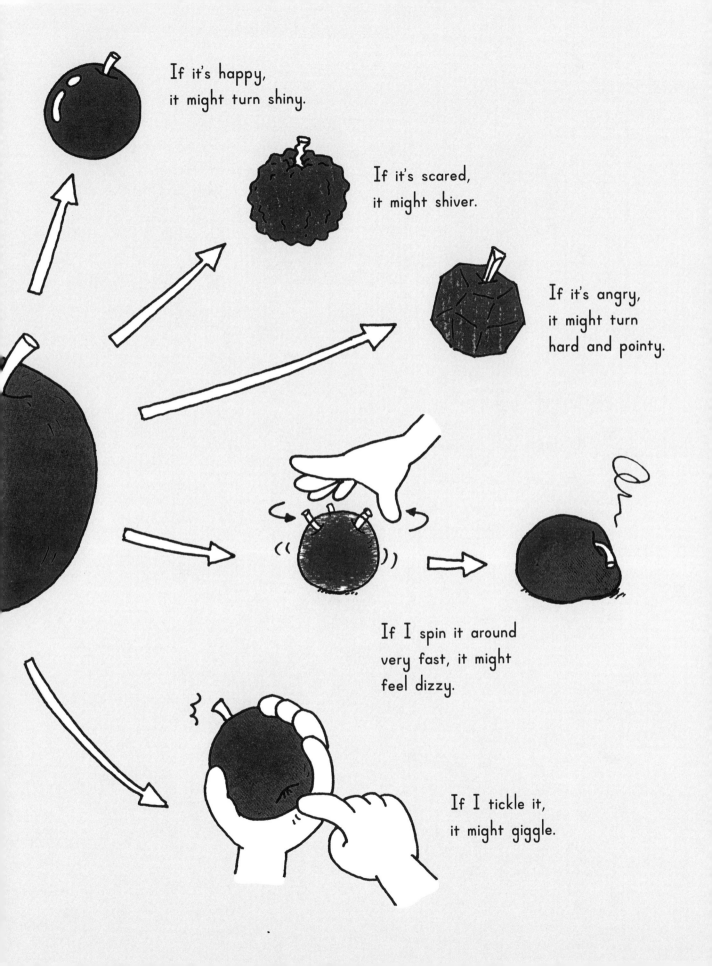

If it's happy,
it might turn shiny.

If it's scared,
it might shiver.

If it's angry,
it might turn
hard and pointy.

If I spin it around
very fast, it might
feel dizzy.

If I tickle it,
it might giggle.

It might be all-knowing.

It might want to learn all about me.

It might have brothers and sisters.

Pearly Apple

Jingo Apple

Dibble Apple

Dotty Apple

Mungo Apple

It might have lots of family and friends.

Billy Jilly Frilly Milly Silly

Rocky Blocky Vicky Tricky Ricky

Dusty Rusty Crusty Twisty Misty

Queenie Greenie Beanie Meanie Teenie

Droopy Scoopy Loopy Hoopy Gloopy

Whirly   Twirly   Curly   Pearly   Shirley

Bingo   Wingo   Jingo

Wibble   Nibble   Squibble   Dibble   Jibble

Knotty   Spotty   Dotty

Mingo   Mongo   Mango   Mungo   Bob

Why is it here in the first place?

Mum might have bought it at the supermarket.

Dad might have brought it home after a night out.

It might be a secret signal.

'You must join our gang!'

It might be my grandma in disguise.

It might be the bait in a trap to catch me.

It might have seen lots of things in
lots of places before it arrived here...

What will the apple do now?

It might take its friends and family
and go back to where it came from.

Everyone might be an apple...

except me!

It might grow arms and legs.

It might start to look like me.

It might roll me into a ball.

It might paint me red.

It might take
my place!

Perhaps I might
as well try eating it.

It might taste like nothing.

It might be very sour.

It might be very spicy.

It might be too hard for my teeth.

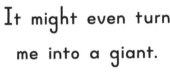
It might stretch
like rubber.

It might fly
like a balloon.

It might even turn
me into a giant.

But what if it's just an apple? It's the right colour, it's not moving, it's not making any weird noises, and I'm getting hungry...

crunch!

munch munch munch

gulp!

Now I know
what it is.

It's delicious!

Translated from the Japanese

First published in the United Kingdom in 2015 by
Thames & Hudson Ltd, 181A High Holborn, London WC1V 7QX

Reprinted in 2016, 2017

Original edition © 2013 Shinsuke Yoshitake / Bronze Publishing, Inc.
This edition © 2015 Thames & Hudson Ltd, London

British Library Cataloguing-in-Publication Data
A catalogue record for this book is available from the British Library

ISBN 978-0-500-65048-6

Printed in Malaysia

To find out about all our publications, please visit **www.thamesandhudson.com**.
There you can subscribe to our e-newsletter, browse or download our current catalogue,
and buy any titles that are in print.